SHINE AND THE CHAOS CREW

The Day of TREACHEROUS TRAVEL

Written by Chris Callaghan

Illustrated by Amit Tayal

Collins

Shinoy and the Chaos Crew

When Shinoy downloads the Chaos Crew app on his phone, a glitch in the system gives him the power to summon his TV heroes into his world.

With the team on board, Shinoy can figure out what dastardly plans the red-eyed S.N.A.I.R., a Super Nasty Artificial Intelligent Robot, has come up with, and save the day.

1 A nice day out

Shinoy was watching the world whizz past
the train window. He was imagining he was on
a spaceship gathering speed, before taking off for
an adventure on the far side of the galaxy.

"Good morning," came
a voice over the loud speaker.
"The buffet car will be
opening soon, where
a range of hot and cold
beverages and a selection
of sandwiches will
be available."

"Are we ready for a nice
family day out?" said
Mum, trying to
sound enthusiastic.
She nodded at Dad,
his face squished against
the window
as he slept.
"Sleeping Beauty
needs some new
walking shoes for
work and we can have
lunch at Lazy Pete's
Pizza Palace."

Shinoy's tummy
rumbled at
the thought.

The speakers crackled into life again. "The next station will be —" A high-pitched squeal interrupted the announcement, and a booming voice vibrated round the carriage: "The Forbidden Zone!"

Passengers glanced at their tickets in confusion.

"S.N.A.I.R.!" Shinoy gasped.

Mum tutted. "If that metal monster spoils our shopping trip, I won't be happy!"

The train sped through the next station leaving travellers open-mouthed on the platform. A passenger who wanted to get off pulled the emergency stop, but the train sped up.

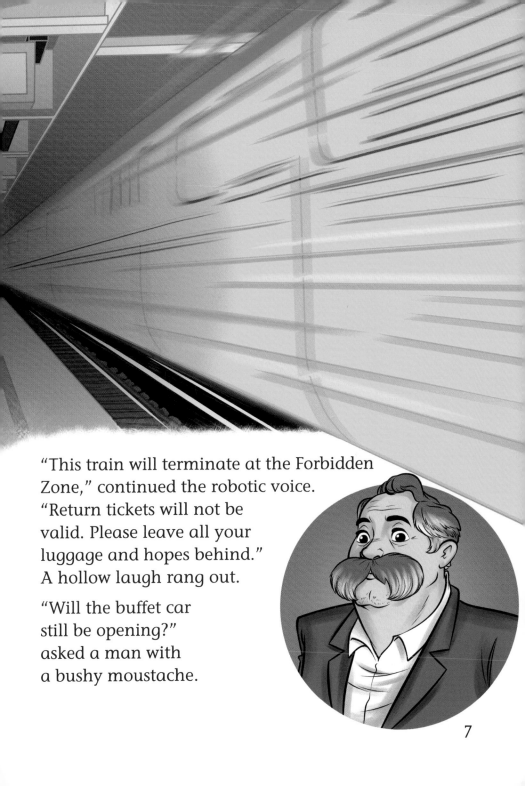

"This train will terminate at the Forbidden Zone," continued the robotic voice. "Return tickets will not be valid. Please leave all your luggage and hopes behind." A hollow laugh rang out.

"Will the buffet car still be opening?" asked a man with a bushy moustache.

Dad woke up with a snort. "Are we nearly there yet?"

"We're going to the Forbidden Zone!" said Myra.

"Oh? Shinoy's favourite comic shop? As long as you spend your own pocket money there."

"No," explained Shinoy, "it's where S.N.A.I.R.'s army was banished at the end of series 3. You can go in, but you never come out!"

"Do your 'action station' thing!" suggested Myra.

Shinoy pressed the special app on his phone. "You mean – Call to Action, Chaos Crew!"

"Yeah, whatever!"

But nothing happened! No Chaos Crew hero stepped out from a flash of light.

Then a familiar face appeared upside down outside the window. Merit waved smartly.

2 Diversion ahead

Shinoy ran towards the train door, but remembered that they locked automatically. How was Merit going to get in?

There was a noise coming from the roof. Shinoy looked up and saw a purple beam of light moving in a circle on the ceiling.

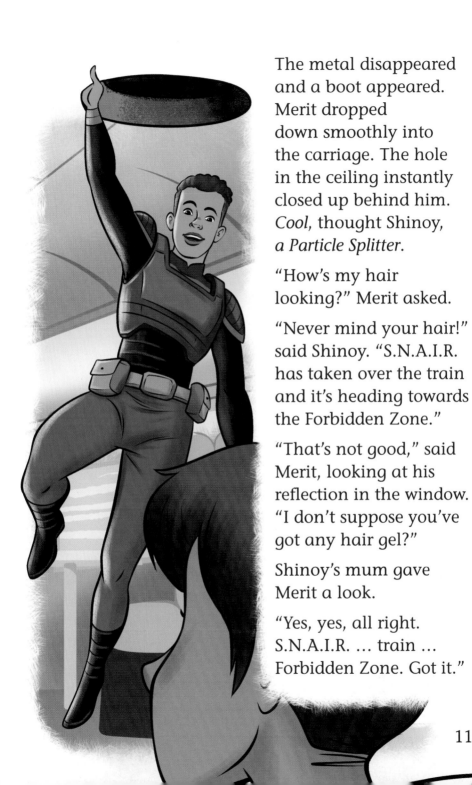

The metal disappeared and a boot appeared. Merit dropped down smoothly into the carriage. The hole in the ceiling instantly closed up behind him. *Cool*, thought Shinoy, *a Particle Splitter*.

"How's my hair looking?" Merit asked.

"Never mind your hair!" said Shinoy. "S.N.A.I.R. has taken over the train and it's heading towards the Forbidden Zone."

"That's not good," said Merit, looking at his reflection in the window. "I don't suppose you've got any hair gel?"

Shinoy's mum gave Merit a look.

"Yes, yes, all right. S.N.A.I.R. ... train ... Forbidden Zone. Got it."

11

"We need to get to the train driver," Shinoy said. Merit agreed.

Lots of passengers were standing up and clogging the aisles.

"OK, people!" Merit called out. "Can everyone please sit down and remain calm?"

They all looked at Merit gormlessly, until he unzipped something from his Chaos Vest and waved it about. "I'm in control of the situation. Look, I have a lanyard."

Everyone reluctantly sat back in their seats.

Merit pointed at Shinoy and Myra. "You two come with me." He handed Shinoy's mum another lanyard. "Keep these good people calm. They'll respect the lanyard."

"What about me?" asked Dad.

"You sit there and look handsome, OK, amigo?"

Dad nodded. "I can do that."

They made their way through the train, but as it thundered into a tunnel, something weird happened. Merit disappeared! Once the train was out of the tunnel, a confused Merit fizzled back into view. Luckily, the passengers were too busy looking out of the windows to notice.

"What happened?" he asked.

Shinoy looked at his phone. "There's no phone reception when we go through a tunnel. I guess that means the connection to your world disconnects, too."

Merit shuddered. "Weird!"

Suddenly, something else weird happened. The carriage juddered and the clickety-clack of the train on the tracks stopped.

3 Take off!

Something didn't feel right and Shinoy's tummy lurched.

"Good morning, ladies and gentlemen," crackled the robotic voice again. "We have successfully taken off. Thank you for flying with S.N.A.I.R. Air."

There was another hollow laugh, followed by the screams of passengers as the train lifted up into the sky.

It didn't take long for the view to turn from trees to grey clouds. The journey through the train became a gruelling climb for the three of them as their path became steeper.

They used the headrests to pull themselves along.

Shinoy stole a look out of the window, and then wished he hadn't. "Faster, Merit!"

The clouds were turning from a familiar grey to an otherworldly crimson.

Once the clouds had cleared, a new and terrifying landscape appeared. Lava-spewing volcanoes filled the skyline, while barren deserts seemed to go on for ever.

Shinoy gulped. "It's the Fields of Fire!"

Merit nodded. "Next stop ... the Forbidden Zone!"

When they reached the driver's cab, the door was locked. Merit drew a purple ring around the lock with the trusty Particle Splitter. The metal peeled back and he slid his arm through the hole and unlocked the door.

S.N.A.I.R. greeted them with his arms wide open. The driver sat in a corner, chained up.

Merit looked at the driver and then back at Shinoy and Myra. "S.N.A.I.R. has not respected the lanyard."

"What took you so long?" S.N.A.I.R. snarled. "Are the prisoners behaving?"

"Prisoners?" asked Myra.

"Forgive me," S.N.A.I.R. replied. "I should've said 'soon-to-be prisoners'! Once we've passed the force field of the Forbidden Zone, there's no way out. And everyone in this rust bucket will spend the rest of their meaningless lives polishing army boots."

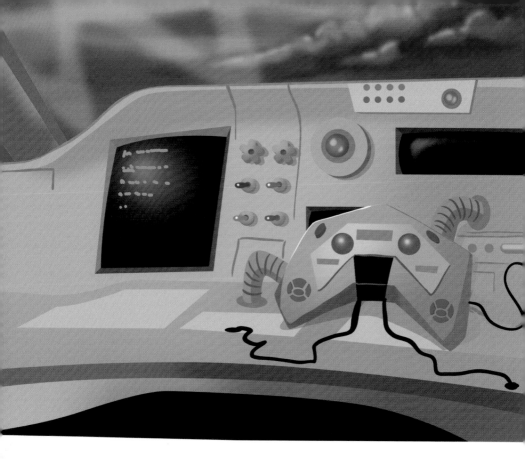

Shinoy felt the train descend and knew their journey was coming to an end. Just then, he noticed a device fitted to the train driver's dashboard. It was a Dimension Drive! A Dimension Drive was capable of moving spaceships between different realities. S.N.A.I.R. was using it to control the train!

"Psst, Merit!" Shinoy angled his head towards the Dimension Drive. "Can we reverse the programming?" he whispered.

Merit's eyes lit up. "Only one way to find out!"

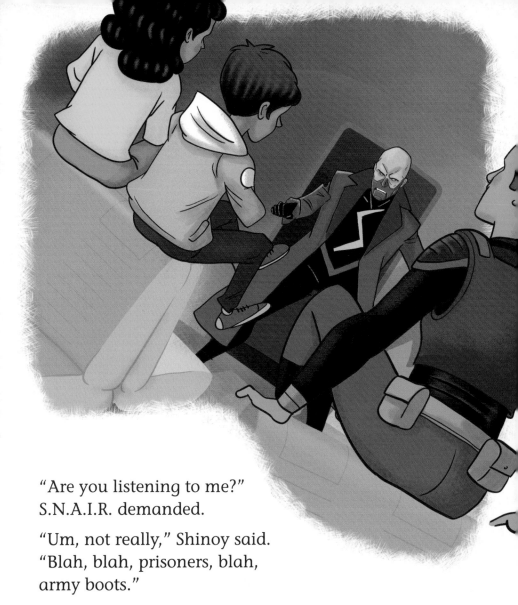

"Are you listening to me?"
S.N.A.I.R. demanded.

"Um, not really," Shinoy said.
"Blah, blah, prisoners, blah,
army boots."

"Once we travel through the ceremonial
Passage of Lost Dignity, we'll arrive at
the boundary of the Forbidden Zone and
the point of no return!"

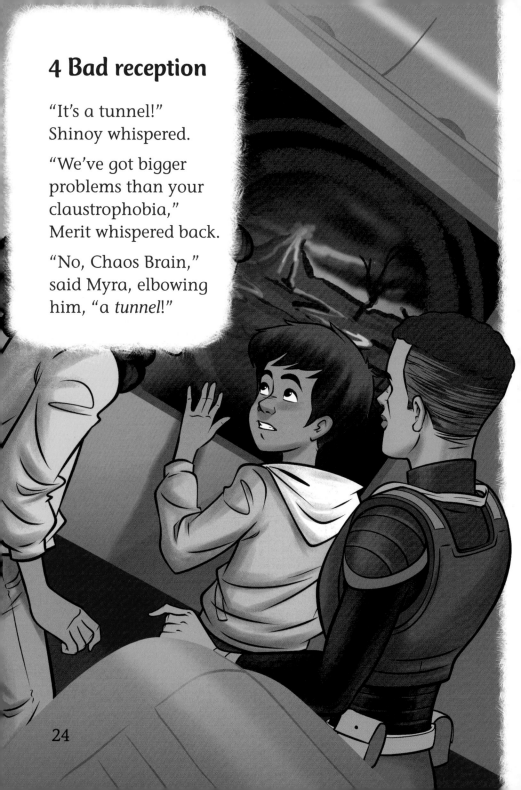

4 Bad reception

"It's a tunnel!" Shinoy whispered.

"We've got bigger problems than your claustrophobia," Merit whispered back.

"No, Chaos Brain," said Myra, elbowing him, "a *tunnel*!"

"Oh!" said Merit. He stepped away from Shinoy. "Sorry, old friends, but I'm not spending the rest of my days scrubbing the filthy boots of Snotty's army. I'm out of here."

The carriage lost its red glow and darkened as they entered the tunnel. Merit pretended to fiddle with his watch and fizzled away into the darkness.

At first, S.N.A.I.R. seemed confused, but then a smile spread across his metal face.

"Oh, this is glorious!" he said, moving closer to Shinoy. "Your precious Chaos Crew hero has deserted you in your time of need. How does that feel?" He bent down so he was face to face with Shinoy. Shinoy wrinkled his nose at the stench of ancient oil.

"I want to see what defeat looks like," he continued, enjoying himself. "I want to see humiliation."

A red glow crept back into the carriage. They were coming out of the tunnel. A purple circle appeared on the side of the carriage. Wild desert was visible through it.

"That isn't possible!" said S.N.A.I.R.

Merit fizzled back into view, right behind S.N.A.I.R. "Good soldiers clean their own boots." A highly polished Chaos Crew boot pressed against their enemy's metallic bottom and pushed him out through the hole. S.N.A.I.R. managed a feeble scream before disappearing.

The hole in the carriage closed sharply.

Merit grabbed the Dimension Drive and reprogrammed it.

"You know how to use that?" asked Myra, as she helped the driver out of his chains.

Shinoy laughed, "Series 2, episodes 3 and 5."

"And don't forget series 3, episode 6!" Merit grinned.

"Why don't we get home first," said Myra, "and then you two can geek-out as much as you like?"

"Good plan," smiled Merit.

The train swayed violently as it turned to avoid the force field.

"Maybe we can find a way back without any tunnels this time?" asked Shinoy.

"I happen to have a Mind Wipe with me," added Merit. "The passengers will just think they've been to West Winton and back."

The man with the bushy moustache appeared at the door. "Is the buffet car open yet?"

"I don't think everyone will need a Mind Wipe," said Shinoy. "Some of them haven't noticed anything!"

All aboard

Ideas for reading

Written by Clare Dowdall, PhD
Lecturer and Primary Literacy Consultant

Reading objectives

- discuss the sequence of events in books and how items of information are related
- make inferences on the basis of what is being said and done
- predict what might happen on the basis of what has been read so far
- explain and discuss their understanding of books, poems and other material, both those that they listen to and those that they read for themselves

Spoken language objectives

- use spoken language to develop understanding through speculating, hypothesising, imagining and exploring ideas
- participate in discussions, presentations, performances and debates

Curriculum links: English – composition: write narratives about fictional experiences; Art – develop art and design techniques

Word count: 1,580

Interest words: buffet car, beverages, emergency stop, aisles, passenger, clickety-clack, lanyard, terminate

Resources: pencils and paper, comic strip grids or ICT for comic strip making, example comic strips

Build a context for reading

- Read the title *The Day of Treacherous Travel* and look at the front cover. Ask children to suggest what the title might mean.
- Read the blurb together. Ask children to develop their ideas about what the title might mean – with reference to the information about the out-of-control train.
- Explain that the story is an adventure story about a train that is hijacked. Read the interest words to the children, and add to it, to build a bank of vocabulary that might be used in a train story.